WEST CHICAGO PUBLIC LIBRARY DISTRICT

3 6653 00180 6144

P9-BUI-930

WITHDRAWN

West Chicago Public Library District
118 West Washington
West Chicago, IL 60185-2803
Phone # (630) 231-1552

The Hinky-Pink

AN OLD TALE RETOLD BY

Megan McDonald

ILLUSTRATED BY Brian Floca

A Richard Jackson Book
Atheneum Books for Young Readers
NEW YORK * LONDON * TORONTO * SYDNEY

B ack when mirrors could talk and princes were frogs, there lived a girl in Old Italy named Anabel.

FIRENZE

Alas, *not* Anabella.

Day after day, Anabel sat in her tiny room hemming and hawing over heaps of mending unending. *Noioso!* Toes of socks. Knees of stockings. Seats of pants. Oh, she might as well sew potato sacks!

Anabel dreamed of the day she'd make a dress fit for a princess. A dress that would dance the tarantella.

Anabel had never even seen a princess. Not one.
But surely princesses had angelic hair and golden
voices and tiny feet. And names that ended in "ella."

Anabel had never worn a glass slipper. Not one.
She had never danced all night or slept on a pea. Never.
And she had never been kissed (by toad or prince). Ever.

But there was one thing (one very princess-y thing)
that Anabel-not-Anabella could do better than any princess.

She could sew faster than a demon, and finer, too. Her
stitches were straight as a new set of teeth. Her French
knots were perfect roses. Her lace, why it was
as wispy as any spider web in the kingdom.
If only she could embroider silk and
satin, touch velvet and voile . . .

Now it's said that inside the Great Castle of Firenze was a room cloaked in velvet. Inside the velvet room was a princess. A princess with three names.

Isabella Caramella Gorgonzola.

The three-name princess did what princesses do. She ate raspberry tarts all day, of course. And on this particular day, she dropped her raspberry tart (*splat!*) on her fanciest dress.

"Holy macaroni!" cried Mag, her nursemaid. "You've gone and ruined another dress."

"Pff!" Isabella said. "I want a new dress, spun from the silk of a thousand silkworms. A dress the color of a ruby snowbird's wing. With sequins that glitter like sparkleberries and stitches as lacey as snowflakes."

Faster than a flea, Mag flew to Anabel's door. A determined *knock-knock* interrupted the girl's daydream. Before you could say "whip stitch," Anabel was tossed like a laundry sack atop a dappled mare and whisked off to the Great Castle, Mag at the reins.

Soon she was led down a year-long hall carpeted in red.

Gilt-framed pictures lined the walls. Crystal lamps glittered like stars. At the end was a velvet room where a girl sat upon piles of satin pillows. The girl did not have angelic hair. She had poodle curls plain as *pennoni*. She did not have a golden voice. It was more of a croak. And she did not have tiny princess feet. Hers were as large as lily pads.

You!

croaked Princess Isabella Caramella Gorgonzola. "What's-Your-Name! Make me the finest dress in all of Firenze. You have one week."

"Holy ratatouille!" cried Anabel. "One week?!"

"Is something wrong with your ears?" snapped the princess. "One week, until the Farfalla."

The Butterfly Ball! Anabel's heart leaped. Why, it was the fanciest ball all year. But one week . . . *impossibile!*

"Take her to the tower at once!" ordered the princess.

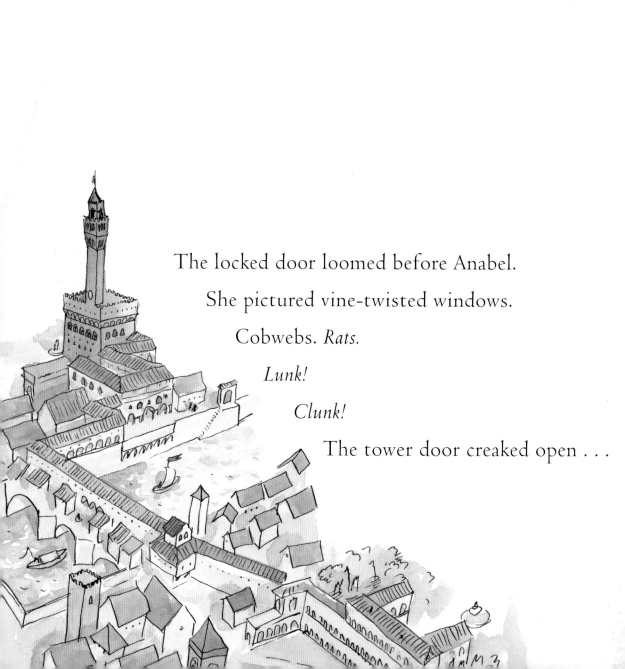

The locked door loomed before Anabel.

She pictured vine-twisted windows.

Cobwebs. *Rats.*

Lunk!

Clunk!

The tower door creaked open . . .

Heaven! Silk, sateen, chiffon, organza, crinoline and crepe. Gold scissors, shiny needles, and thread clear as glass. Even the thimble was silver!

"Holy pincushions!" cried Anabel.

"Get some rest," said Mag. "And set to work straightaway come morn."

Anabel did. Never had she slept such a dreamy sleep,
under mountains of covers, atop clouds of pillows.

That is, until something went . . .

PINCH

Anabel awoke with a start in the middle of the night. She cried,

aargh!

as all the covers were thrashed about and snatched right from her bed.

Anabel crawled back into bed. But no sooner had she pulled the covers on tight and drifted back to sleep than she felt another *PINCH!*

AARGH! The covers were a tangled knot on the floor. Again!

Anabel chased about the room with a broom. She tore open cupboards, tossed aside taffeta, threw open curtains. She poked under tables, peered under rugs, pried open chests.

"Show yourself!" she shouted.

Still nothing.

No one.

If she made the bed once,
she made it sixty times that night.

The next morning, Mag took one look at the tornado of a room and cried, "*Che confusione!* What a mess! What on earth happened here?"

"I didn't get a wink of sleep! Just look at my stitches. A dungeon full of dressmakers could not finish this dress on time."

Mag wagged her finger and clucked her tongue. "The barking of dogs does not reach heaven."

"I think I'm bewitched!" cried Anabel.

"Nonsense," said Mag. "You'll just have to work twice as fast now. Half the day is gone."

Snip, snip, snip. Sew, sew… ZZZZZ. Anabel tried to make her cross-stitch look like snowflakes, but it turned to cauliflower.

Santo cielo!

And so it went, the second night of sewing, and the third. Poor Anabel! She stayed up till two snipping and stitching because she couldn't sleep. And she couldn't sleep because some*one*, or some*thing*, pinched her and stole her covers each night.

Anabel tied the covers to the bedposts. She weighted all four corners with rocks. She piled chairs around the bed. But no matter what she did, some*ONE*, or some*THING*, wrestled her covers to the floor.

After three nights of no sleep, Anabel's diamond eyelet did not look like blooming chrysanthemums. More like wilted parsley. Her seams were wrinkled as chicken skins, and her hems zigzagged like chimney smoke. Her wide Gobelin stitch looked like a goblin itself got hold of it.

"Dear oh dear!" cried Mag.
"I dare say you've got yourself a
Hinky-Pink! The dress will *never* be
done in time for the ball! Not with
a Hinky-Pink!"

"A Hinky-Pink?!"

"A Hinky-Pink is a hudgin," Mag whispered.

"*Mamma mia!* What in the world is a *hudgin*?"
asked Anabel.

"A hudgin is a hobbledy-gob," said Mag,
looking over her shoulder.

"Well, this hudgin, hobbledy-gob, *Hinky-Pink* is stealing my covers every night until I'm chill as a fish and can't sew a stitch!"

Mag clucked her tongue again and plucked at her chin hairs. "Hudgins! Hobbledy-gobs! Hinky-Pinks!" She flew from the room, apron slapping, braids flapping.

That evening, Mag returned with Anabel's supper. "I've been to see the Wise Woman. There is only one thing to do. You must make this Hinky-Pink a bed of its own. Then it'll no longer have to steal *your* covers."

So that very night Anabel pushed a high table against the wall and pulled down velvet curtains for covers. "At last, the Hinky-Pink shall have its own bed, and I, a good night's sleep!"

at last!

Just as she was about to dream a dreamy dream, Anabel heard a moaning and a groaning.

Too high and too hard!
Too high and too hard!

PINCH

Her bedclothes twisted and tangled and fell in a knot to the ground.

So Anabel piled a heap of the softest eiderdown quilts in the corner. "I'm not afraid of some old hobbledy-gob, Hinky-Pink. Here's a bed for you. Now let me get some sleep!"

But as soon as she drifted off, a voice moaned
and groaned:

Too soft and too slippery!
Too soft and too slippery!

PINCH

Off went Anabel's covers, even though
she'd tucked them in as tight as the skin on an apple.

Every night Anabel made a new bed for the Hinky-Pink.

She made a bed in the far corner of a cupboard.

Too dark and
too deep!
Too dark and
too deep!

She slung some of her satin from hook to hook
across the room.

Too long and too loose!
Too long and too loose!

She even tried making the thing a cradle.

Too teeter and too
totter!

Too teeter and too
totter!

On the very day before the dance, Mag shook
Anabel awake. "Holy *portaspilli*! Wake up, child!
Tomorrow night is the Butterfly Ball. The
princess must have her dress."

"But . . . the Hinky-Pink! My lace looks like cheesecloth. My hems look like saddle cinches. And I have yet to sew a single sequin on the butterfly sash!"

"Stay up all night if you must!" said Mag. "Do the best you can—walk with your slippers until you find your shoes."

Anabel rubbed her eyes. She picked up her sewing, threaded her needle, slipped on her thimble, and . . .

Wait just a minute!

Could it be . . . ?

Why ever not? she thought. *I've tried everything else.*

She lined the thimble with her silkiest
satin. She added peach down for a pillow
and a rose petal for a blanket.

Anabel set the thimble on the windowsill.
Before she could climb into bed herself, she
heard a most happy humming.

There, in the thimble, was a dot. A speck. No
bigger than a French knot.

"*You're* the *Hinky-Pink*?" said Anabel, laughing so
hard she got hiccups. "Why, you're no bigger than a
flea! I shall have to call you Thimbelina."

She tucked herself into bed. As she shut her eyes,
the Hinky-Pink whispered:

Just so. Just so.
I like a bed made just so!
A bed fit for a princess.
Fit for a queen. Stupendo!

Anabel fell to sleep without a *PINCH!* She slept
to the tune of the tiny humming. *La la la la la la!* She
slept the sleep of a princess without a pea. She slept
the sleep of a hundred years.

When she awoke, she began to sew. *Snip, snip, snip.*
She sewed all day, faster than a demon, and finer,
too. As the last stitch was stitched and the last knot
knotted, Anabel was whisked off to the princess's
chambers, thread and thimble in hand.

Princess Isabella Caramella Gorgonzola closed her eyes and held her hands high in the air while three maids hustle-bustled to slip the dress over her head in a rustle of silk. The princess was primped and puffed and poofed and fluffed. And when all the poofing was just so, Isabella took a look in the mirror.

Anabel held her breath. Making the dress was a dream come true. But what if it looked like an old potato sack on the princess?

The princess began to laugh. A lovely laugh, more music than toad. And when she laughed, her nose wrinkled and her eyes twinkled and her sequins winked in the light until the whole room glowed a little brighter.

Bellissima!

Anabel watched her dress float down the hall.
To think! She, Anabel-not-Anabella, had made a
dress that was on its way *to the ball*. A dress that
would dance the tarantella.

With each swish of the princess's skirts, the butterfly sash seemed to flutter its wings. And in the eye of the butterfly was something only the dressmaker herself noticed.

A dot? A speck?

A most unusual French knot . . .

or was it?

AUTHOR'S NOTE

The Hinky-Pink was inspired by the tale *The Bed Just So* by Margery Bailey in the book *Whistle for Good Fortune* (Little, Brown and Company, 1940). It was later retold by Jeanne B. Hardendorff (Four Winds Press, 1975). I have restored the tale to its original setting (Firenze, Old Italy) and style, but the invention of the princess tale is mine, and the original story featured a tailor rather than a young seamstress. Librarians the world over love to tell this tale aloud, and I first heard it told at the Carnegie Library in Pittsburgh, PA, where I once had my beginnings as a children's librarian and storyteller.

—*M. M.*

ILLUSTRATOR'S NOTE

Readers should note that *The Hinky-Pink* is no substitute for a reputable art history survey. Still, if you are lucky enough to visit Florence, there are some buildings here that you will recognize. Florence's immense Palazzo Pitti stands in for the book's Great Castle of Firenze. Palazzo Vecchio, which connects to the Pitti via the winding, Arno River–hopping Vasari Corridor, sports the soaring tower in which Anabel is locked. And seen often in the background here, as in the city itself, is the dome of the beautiful Santa Maria del Fiore—the Duomo, or cathedral, of Florence.

—*B. F.*

For Amy Kellman — *M. M.*   *   For my nieces, Lauren and Natalie — *B. F.*

Atheneum Books for Young Readers · An imprint of Simon & Schuster Children's Publishing Division
1230 Avenue of the Americas, New York, New York 10020 · Text copyright © 2008 by Megan McDonald
Illustrations copyright © 2008 by Brian Floca · All rights reserved, including the right of reproduction in whole
or in part in any form. · Book design by Michael McCartney · The text for this book is set in Venetian 301.
The illustrations for this book are rendered in watercolor and ink. · Manufactured in China
10 9 8 7 6 5 4 3
Library of Congress Cataloging-in-Publication Data · McDonald, Megan
The Hinky Pink / retold by Megan McDonald ; illustrated by Brian Floca. — 1st ed. · p. cm.
"A Richard Jackson Book." · Summary: Summoned to the Great Castle of Firenze to create a special dress
for Princess Isabella Caramella Gorgonzola, Anabel, a talented seamstress, is at first delighted but then
increasingly despairing as time passes and her efforts are continually subverted by an unseen sprite.
ISBN-13: 978-0-689-87588-5 · ISBN-10: 0-689-87588-6
[1. Fairy tales. 2. Dressmakers—Fiction. 3. Goblins—Fiction. 4. Princesses—Fiction.]
I. Floca, Brian, ill. II. Title. · PZ8.M4577 Hin · [Fic]—dc22 · 2007004698